THE
TOTALLY NINJA
RACCOONS
AND THE
SECRET OF
THE CANYON

by Kevin Coolidge

Illustrated by Jubal Lee

Be a reading ninja!

Kevin Coolidge

The Totally Ninja Raccoons Are:

Rascal:
He's the shortest
brother and loves
doughnuts. He's
great with his paws
and makes really
cool gadgets. He's a
little goofy and loves
both his brothers,
even when they pick
on him, but maybe
not right then.

Bandit:
He's the oldest
brother. He's tall
and lean. He's
super smart and
loves to read. He
leads the Totally
Ninja Raccoons,
but he couldn't do
it by himself.

Kevin:
He may be the
middle brother,
but he refuses to be
stuck in the middle.
He has the moves
and the street smarts
that the Totally
Ninja Raccoons are
going to need, even
if it does sometimes
get them into trouble
as well as out of
trouble.

CONTENTS

1. Take a Hike   page 1

2. Legend of the Crying Baby   page 7

3. Legend has It   page 13

4. Secret Meeting   page 17

5. The Water's Edge   page 21

6. Sink or Swim   page 25

7. Saving the Beast for Last   page 29

8. Pieces of Eight   page 33

"Wait up, guys! I have short legs!"

1

TAKE A HIKE

Deep in the woods, Bandit brushes aside a fern as he leads the hike. Behind him, Kevin uses his staff to whack branches. Rascal struggles to keep up after adjusting the straps on his backpack.

"Are we there yet?" puffs Rascal.

"We have another two kilometers before we get to Barbour's Rock," answers Bandit.

Kevin and Rascal stop walking and plop down on the ground. Bandit puts his paws on his hips and stares at his lazy brothers.

"Are you guys just going to just sit there?" asks Bandit.

"Two kilometers? I thought you said it was just a little over a mile?" complains Kevin.

"A kilometer is a unit of measure from the metric system. It's equal to sixty percent of a mile," says Bandit.

"That's confusing," says Rascal.

"I don't see why we don't just make our own measurement system," says Kevin.

"Because if everyone made up their own measurements, then nobody's would be the same," answers Bandit.

"No problem. I'd let them use mine," says Kevin.

"I have short legs. My measurements would be short. I need to rest longer, and I need a cold birch beer," says Rascal.

"We just started hiking this trail," says Bandit.

"But we walked ten miles from town to get here!" shout Kevin and Rascal.

"This shouldn't be easy. We're training to be ninjas," says Bandit. He pauses and sees how tired his brothers are. "Oh, OK, rest five minutes and make sure you hydrate. That means water and **not** birch beer," says Bandit.

Kevin and Rascal dig through their backpacks. Kevin gets out a water bottle, and Rascal gets out water and a candy bar.

"Hey, you have any more of those?" asks Kevin.

"This is my last one," says Rascal with his mouth full of candy bar.

"Rascal, if you didn't bring enough for everyone..." Bandit starts to say.

"I need to keep my energy up," says Rascal.

"If you keep this up, I'm going to..." says Kevin.

"Shhhh, both of you! Do you hear that?" asks Bandit.

Kevin and Rascal stop their bickering and listen.

"I don't hear anything," says Kevin.

"It was probably just Bigfoot," says Rascal.

"You can't hear Bigfoot. He's super-sneaky," says Kevin.

"And we **still** caught him," says Rascal.

"We totally caught him," says Kevin.

"What if it's a bear?" asks Rascal.

"Shhh, there it is again," says Bandit.

The raccoons tilt their heads to listen. There is a sound. It's really faint.

"It sounds like a baby crying," says Bandit.

"Yeah, he probably didn't want to go on a hike either," says Rascal.

"We should check it out!" says Kevin.

"It sounds like a human baby. That's not our job," says Rascal.

"What if something bad has happened to the parents?" asks Bandit.

"Let's go!" says Kevin.

Kevin and Bandit take off running into the woods towards the noise. Rascal puts his backpack on, and starts to follow.

"Wait up, guys! I have short legs!" shouts Rascal.

"You haven't heard the legend of the crying baby?"

2

LEGEND OF THE CRYING BABY

The Ninja Raccoons come to the end of the path. There's a huge rock on the edge of a large canyon. Kevin and Bandit stop and look around.

"Where's Rascal?" asks Bandit.

"He was right behind me," says Kevin.

Rascal comes huffing out of the woods. He stops and puts his paws on his knees. He's panting and sweating. Raccoons can do both. It helps regulate their body temperature.

"Why didn't you guys wait up for me?" complains Rascal.

"Someone needs our help!" says Kevin.

"I don't hear anything," says Rascal.

The raccoons stop talking and listen, but there doesn't seem to be anything but the chirping of a nearby cricket.

"There, can you hear it? It's really faint," says Bandit.

"It sounds like it's coming from down in the canyon," says Kevin.

Rascal walks to the edge and looks down.

"I don't hear anything," says Rascal.

A deep voice comes from out of the woods.

"You won't hear anything at all if you get too close to the edge," says the voice.

Rascal takes a look down, shivers, and takes a big step back.

"How are you doing tonight, Bigfoot?" asks Bandit.

A hairy, little creature steps out of the woods. He's not very tall, but he sure has huge feet.

"I'm great. I love hiking at the Pennsylvania Grand Canyon," says Bigfoot.

"Did you hear a baby crying?" asks Kevin.

"You heard it?" says Bigfoot.

"Of course we heard it. We're ninjas," says Bandit.

"Not everyone hears the Indian baby crying," says Bigfoot.

"Indian baby?" says Bandit.

"You haven't heard the legend of the crying baby?" asks Bigfoot.

"Legend? Ohhh, tell me, tell us!" shouts Rascal.

Rascal, Bandit, and Kevin all gather around Bigfoot to hear the legend of the crying baby.

"Several hundred years ago, the only humans here were known as the Lenape. They were the Native Americans that lived in what would one day become Tioga County. This area was lush and green and there were even more trees than today, but there was a long drought, and the woods dried up," says Bigfoot.

"What happened?" asks Rascal.

"There was a long time without rain, and there was fire after fire. The fires were so bad that many of the animals got burned up, and a lot of the Bigfeet moved away," says Bigfoot.

"Is that why there are so few of you around?" asks Kevin.

"That's one reason," says Bigfoot.

"Well, what does this have to do with a baby?" asks Bandit.

9

"One of the Indian mothers would come to this very spot to wish for rain. She wasn't eating very much because the fire burned the woods where they caught and gathered their food," says Bigfoot.

"She should have just gone to the Chinese restaurant and gotten some General Tso's chicken," says Rascal.

"That was before there were any restaurants. You had to catch your own food," says Bigfoot.

"Like crayfish?" asks Kevin.

"Or venison--that's deer meat. Anyway, the Indian mother was tired and hungry, and she slipped and fell off the edge of the canyon with her baby. The mother and child landed on a ledge, and the baby cried until they were rescued," says Bigfoot.

"That's terrifying!" says Bandit.

"It was very sad. Sometimes on a warm summer night, if you listen closely, you can still hear that baby crying...," says Bigfoot.

"That's scary!" says Rascal.

"It's kind of creepy," says Kevin.

"We need to investigate this further," says Bandit.

Kevin and Rascal both shake their heads and moan.

"I'd be careful. There are some parts of the canyon where the Indians wouldn't go," warns Bigfoot.

"Nothing scares us," replies Bandit.

"I heard that Gypsy--the Cat--is looking for you," warns Bigfoot.

"I wonder if she wants those parts back?" says Bandit.

"Didn't you use them in your glove launching system?" says Kevin.

"She can't have them back, because I used them to fix the toaster," says Rascal.

"I like toast," says Kevin.

"Yum, with strawberry jam," says Rascal.

"Come on guys! What are we?" shouts Bandit.

Rascal and Kevin look at each other, and shrug their shoulders.

"Hungry?" say Kevin and Rascal.

"The Ninja Raccoons, remember?" says Bandit.

11

Rascal turns towards Kevin and sticks out his tongue,
and gives Kevin a ripe, juicy raspberry.

3

LEGEND HAS IT

The Ninja Raccoons are in their top secret clubhouse. Bandit reads a book called *Ghosts in Penn's Woods*. Kevin lies in his hammock eating a candy bar and drinking water. Rascal sits at the table tinkering with a funnel.

"I still didn't hear anything," says Rascal.

Rascal holds the funnel up to his ear.

"You couldn't hear anything over your huffing and puffing," says Kevin.

Rascal turns towards Kevin and sticks out his tongue making a juicy raspberry sound.

"Thhhhhhp," says Rascal.

"I heard that," says Kevin.

"I've been reading about the legend of the crying baby. It's different from the one Bigfoot told, but several humans have heard the crying baby," says Bandit.

"I told you we should have just gone to Packer Park and played. I mean, trained on the monkey bars," says Kevin.

"I think we need to investigate the canyon," says Bandit.

"I'm working on my bionic ear. This time I'll hear the baby for sure," says Rascal.

"Bigfoot warned us that there are places the Indians wouldn't go," says Kevin.

"Aren't you curious?" asks Bandit.

"Curiosity is for cats," says Kevin.

"Exactly, don't you want to find out before Gypsy the Cat does?" says Bandit.

"Yes, but I'm taking a flashlight," says Kevin.

"You can use my new solar-powered flashlight!" says Rascal.

"Are you afraid of the dark?" asks Bandit.

"No, of what's hiding in the dark," replies Kevin.

"You'll be safe carrying my flashlight," says Rascal.

"That depends on how fast I carry it," mumbles Kevin.

"Those Ninja Raccoons are going to be totally taken care of..."

4

SECRET MEETING

Meanwhile, at a super-secret location... Gypsy, a large—no, make that very fat--calico cat, sits at the head of a long table. Around the table sit various cats from around the globe. She impatiently looks around.

It's a meeting of the Cat Board: the super-duper, secret organization of felines that plot to take over the world. Cats are sitting around the table quietly talking to each other.

"I meow call to order this meeting of the Cat Board," yowls Gypsy.

The cats are silent once Gypsy starts to talk.

"We are here to discuss my plans on global domination. Uhh, I mean the Cat Board's idea of putting cats in control of everything," says Gypsy.

A Siamese cat looks at Gypsy suspiciously with slanted eyes.

"I don't remember anyone putting you in charge?" purrs the Siamese.

"Oh, yes, I decided. I mean, everyone voted that I should be head of the Cat Board," says Gypsy.

A Persian cat speaks up.

"I don't remember that," says the Persian cat.

"Oh, it was before you got here. Don't be late next time. Anyway, on to business. I need--I mean we need--to take care of a little problem," says Gypsy.

A big, Irish cat speaks up.

"I've heard of your little problem, and I think you should take care of it yourself," says the big, black cat.

"This is a situation that is going to take the full resources of the Cat Board," says Gypsy.

A slim, black and white cat, that looks like it is wearing a tuxedo, speaks up.

"Is it those darn Samurai Possums?" asks the little cat.

"No, it's those meddling Totally Ninja Raccoons. They are a menace to my--I mean our--plans," complains Gypsy.

A nearly hairless cat speaks up.

"Why don't you just unleash your robot guards?" asks the nearly hairless cat.

"Uhh, I'm waiting on some parts," says Gypsy.

"Can't we find someone else to take care of them?" asks the Siamese.

"I placed an ad in the *Wellsboro Gazette*, but everyone actually wanted to be paid," says Gypsy.

"The nerve of people," says the black cat.

"This calls for our latest secret weapon," says the tuxedo cat.

"Mutated spiders?" asks the Persian.

"Spiders are creepy. Uggh, and those sticky webs. I hate spiders," says the hairless cat.

"Exactly, real spiders are icky. We are going to use robotic spiders," says the tuxedo cat.

"Didn't we do that last year?" asks the Persian cat.

"These ones fly!" says the tuxedo cat.

"Ohhhh, coooool!" meow all the cats in the room.

"Those Ninja Raccoons are going to be totally taken care of...," says Gypsy.

"Maybe you should tell that flock of bugs that spiders don't fly!"

5

THE WATER'S EDGE

The Ninja Raccoons navigate over rocks and stones, batting away the ferns and weeds that grow along Pine Creek, the creek that flows through the Pennsylvania Grand Canyon.

"The book says the crying baby is most often heard near Barbour's Rock, which is directly above us," says Bandit.

"We're pretty close to the rapids," says Kevin.

"We need to be careful and not get too close. Barbour's Rock is named for a man that drowned in the rapids," warns Bandit.

"What was that, Bandit?" asks Rascal.

A lone trout rises to the surface of Pine Creek to snatch a large bug flying close to the water.

"Will you make sure to tell Rascal to be careful near the water's edge? He can't hear a single thing I say with that device crammed in his ear," says Bandit.

"I still can't hear the baby. I just hear a buzzing sound!" shouts Rascal.

"Maybe, if you took that thing out of your ear, you could hear us!" shouts Kevin.

"I can't hear you. There's a bionic ear in my ear," says Rascal.

Kevin reaches over and pulls out the bionic ear.

"Can you hear me now?" asks Kevin.

The trout surfaces and quickly spits out a big, hairy and ugly bug with more than the usual six legs.

"I still hear the buzzing in my ear. It sounds like a swarm of mosquitoes," says Rascal.

"Or maybe a flock of flying spiders?!" shouts Kevin who is looking frantically around, alarmed.

"Don't be silly. Spiders can't fly," laughs Bandit.

Rascal points to a large swarm of bugs.

"Maybe you should tell that flock of bugs that spiders don't fly!" shouts Rascal.

"Spiders are NOT bugs. They are arachnids, and a group of spiders is called a cluster or a clutter, not a flock," corrects Bandit.

"Ouch! They're biting me!" shouts Kevin.

"They're flyders!" shouts Rascal.

Kevin swats a big, winged spider on his arm. Bandit and

Rascal start waving their arms around, and swatting spiders, or flyders, as Rascal has named them.

"There are too many of them. We need to make a run for it," says Kevin.

"Into the water! I bet the flyders can't swim," says Bandit.

"Neither can I!" shouts Rascal.

"Jump!" shouts Kevin.

The Ninja Raccoons jump into Pine Creek. Bandit and Kevin dive to avoid the cluster of flyders. Rascal is spluttering around in the water. He's heading towards the rapids.

Kevin and Bandit surface upstream.

"Where's Rascal?" asks Bandit.

"He's heading towards the rapids!" shouts Kevin.

Kevin and Bandit start swimming towards Rascal.

"Hang in there, Rascal!" encourages Bandit.

"Hurry!" Glub-glub noises issue from Rascal's throat as he shouts, "Help! I can't swim!"

Rascal's head disappears below the surface right before the rapids, and he doesn't come back up.

"Hey, guys, what are you doing?"

6

SINK OR SWIM

Kevin and Rascal frantically swim towards the area where Rascal went under.

"Do you see him anywhere?" asks Bandit.

Kevin and Bandit are being swarmed by the flyders. Kevin waves his arms, treading water, and trying to look for Rascal.

"I can't see anything with these bugs," says Kevin.

"Arachnids, but I think they are robotic arachnids," says Bandit.

"Someone took the time to make robotic spiders? That's even creepier," says Kevin.

"Rascal must have gotten sucked into the rapids. We have to go after him," says Bandit.

A tree branch floats between Bandit and Kevin. Kevin grabs hold of the branch.

"Get to the tree branch, Bandit!" shouts Kevin.

The two ninja raccoons are swept into the rapids and go for a bumpy ride. White water and waves are all around the raccoons. The tree branch is tossed all over, and you can't see the raccoon brothers.

The branch makes it through the rapids, coming out on the other side and floating gently in the creek. Little black paws wrapped around the branch.

Bandit and Kevin pull themselves up out of the water. Bandit is dripping wet. Kevin surfaces and spits a mouthful of water at Bandit.

"You see anything?" asks Kevin.

"Not with a face full of water," says Bandit.

"Good news is that we seem to have lost those flying pests," says Kevin.

"The bad news is, where's Rascal? We need to find him as soon as possible!" says Bandit.

Kevin and Bandit are frantically looking for Rascal when a lone raccoon starts waving at them from the shore.

"Hey, guys, what are you doing?" asks Rascal.

"Looking for you!" shout Kevin and Bandit.

"I've been waiting for you guys," says Rascal.

"How did you make it through the rapids?" asks Kevin.

"I thought you couldn't swim?" says Bandit.

"I can't. I stood up and the water was only up to my waist. Pine Creek isn't very deep this time of year," says Rascal.

"You could have said something," says Kevin.

"You guys can swim. Besides, I finally heard the crying baby. It's over this way. Come on!" says Rascal.

Kevin and Bandit exit the river soaking wet, and walk over to where Rascal is waiting.

"There, can you hear it?" says Rascal excitedly.

"If we all push, we can get it standing again."

7

SAVING THE BEAST FOR LAST

The Totally Ninja Raccoons are excited. Everyone can finally hear the crying baby. It doesn't sound too far away.

"I hear it, but it sounds different," says Kevin.

"Probably just because we are in the canyon, and not above," says Bandit.

"It doesn't sound too far away! Let's hurry!" shouts Rascal.

The raccoon brothers go running through the woods. They push through some branches and Mountain Laurel and there, lying on the ground, is a huge, ugly creature with a horn growing out of its head. The creature is crying.

"What is that?!" asks Rascal.

"I have no idea!" shouts Kevin.

"I believe it is a sidehill gouger. I didn't think they were real. I read about them in a book," says Bandit.

"You didn't think werewolves were real," says Rascal.

"Or Bigfoot," says Kevin.

"The book said they live on the side of mountains or steep hills. Their right legs are very short because they are always uphill, and their left legs are very long because they are always pointed downhill," says Bandit.

"It's crying. We should help it," says Rascal.

"Are you crazy? Look at the size of those claws," says Kevin.

"It must have fallen. It can't stand on level ground. It'll starve if we leave it like that," says Bandit.

The Ninja Raccoons approach the sidehill gouger. Rascal gently puts his paw on its side, and it stops crying.

"If we all push, we can get it standing again," says Rascal.

"We can do this," says Bandit.

The three raccoons join together in pushing. The gouger is big and heavy. It's hard work, but by pushing together, the raccoons are able to get the animal standing again.

"We did it!" shouts Kevin.

"Of course, because we are..." says Bandit.

"The Totally Ninja Raccoons!" shout the three brothers.

The sidehill gouger is startled by the noise and runs off up the slope of the canyon and is soon out of sight.

"The mystery of the crying baby is solved!" shouts Bandit.

"I knew there was nothing to be afraid of," says Kevin.

"Let's go fishing! I caught one of those flyders. Let's see if we can catch a nice trout," says Rascal.

Rascal holds up a glass jar with a big, ugly flyder crawling around inside.

"Uggh, why don't we just go get some General Tso's chicken," says Kevin.

"And a fortune cookie?" asks Rascal.

"And some of those powdery Chinese doughnuts, because fortune favors family," Bandit smiles.

"Your plan was a stupid idea!" yowls the Siamese cat.

8

PIECES OF EIGHT

"Your plan was a stupid idea!" yowls the Siamese cat.

Gypsy looks disdainfully at the noisy cat. "You know nothing! It was Huck's fault for not waterproofing the flying spiders!" complains Gypsy.

"They were robotic, flying spiders. They were designed to fly, not go underwater! I'm also calling them flyders from now on, because it's a great name. I wish I had thought of it," says the black and white cat.

"I call them a failure, and there are no more flyders! They were all destroyed!" meows Gypsy.

Finn, an all black cat speaks up, "It doesn't matter who's to blame."

"The Ninja Raccoons need to be stopped!" says the Persian cat.

"I have a plan that will fix those meddling raccoons once and for all!" meows Gypsy.

"You've meowed that before," says the Siamese cat.

"This plan will work for sure. We'll do something evil, and blame the raccoons for it, and animal control will do our dirty work for us," says Gypsy proudly.

A nearly hairless cat speaks up, "That will never happen. Doing something bad sounds like hard work," complains the cat.

"Are we not cats? We'll get someone or some **thing** to do it for us," says Gypsy.

"This plan better work, Gypsy. You can be replaced as head of the Cat Board," meows the Siamese cat.

"You'll see," cackles Gyspy," You'll see."

THE END

About the Author

Kevin resides in Wellsboro, just a short hike from the Pennsylvania Grand Canyon. When he's not writing, you can find him at *From My Shelf Books & Gifts*, an independent bookstore he runs with his wife, several helpful employees, and two friendly cats, Huck & Finn.

He's recently become an honorary member of the Cat Board, and when he's not scooping the litter box, or feeding Gypsy her tuna, he's writing more stories about the Totally Ninja Raccoons. Be sure to catch their next big adventure, *The Totally Ninja Raccoons Meet the Thunderbird*.

You can write him at:

From My Shelf Books & Gifts
7 East Ave., Suite 101
Wellsboro, PA 16901

www.wellsborobookstore.com

About the Illustrator

Jubal Lee is a former Wellsboro resident who now resides in sunny Florida, due to his extreme allergic reaction to cold weather.

He is an eclectic artist who, when not drawing raccoons, werewolves, and the like, enjoys writing, bicycling, and short walks on the beach.

About the Sidehill Gouger

The sidehill gouger is a creature of Pennsylvania folklore. These mysterious plant eaters adapted to living on steep hillsides by having legs on one side of their body shorter than the legs on the opposite side. This allows them to stand upright and walk on the sides of mountains.

It's claimed that both left-legged and right-legged gougers exist. The legs of a left-legged gouger are shorter on the left. Right-legged gougers are just the opposite. sidehill gougers always move in the same direction. If they try to reverse direction, they topple over.

If by accident a sidehill gouger falls down a hill, it can't stand up because of its uneven legs. The sidehill gouger could then be easily be captured or starve to death without a helping hand, or paw.

Besides the unusual length of the gouger's legs, little is actually known about the appearance of this animal. Some say it looks like a badger. Some say it looks like a goat. Some say it has huge claws and an ugly horn growing out of its forehead.

What do you think a sidehill gouger looks like? Are sidehill gougers real, or are they just stories and legends? Become a reading ninja, and decide for yourself.

CPSIA information can be obtained
at www.ICGtesting.com
Printed in the USA
LVHW091602070720
659996LV00003B/606